WHATEVER NEXT!

This book belongs to

_____

Also by Jill Murphy
and published by Macmillan

Peace at Last

On the Way Home

WHATEVER NEXT!

JILL MURPHY

MACMILLAN
CHILDREN'S BOOKS

First published 1983 by Macmillan Children's Books
a division of Macmillan Publishers Limited
20 New Wharf Road
London N1 9RR
Basingstoke and Oxford
www.panmacmillan.com
Associated companies worldwide

Revised edition published 1995

ISBN 0 333 63622 8 (HB)
ISBN 0 333 63621 X (PB)

17

A CIP catalogue record for this book is available
from the British Library.

Printed and bound in Belgium

"Can I go to the moon?" asked Baby Bear.

"No you can't," said Mrs Bear.
"It's bathtime.
Anyway, you'd have to find a rocket first."

Baby Bear found a rocket
in the cupboard under the stairs.

He found a space-helmet
on the draining board in the kitchen,
and a pair of space-boots on the
mat by the front door.

He packed his teddy
and some food for the journey
and took off up the chimney . . .

... WHOOSH! Out into the night.

An owl flew past.

"That's a smart rocket," he said.

"Where are you off to?"

"The moon," said Baby Bear.

"Would you like to come too?"

"Yes please," said the owl.

An aeroplane roared out of the clouds.
Baby Bear waved and
some of the passengers waved back.

On and on they flew,
up and up, above the clouds,
past millions of stars till
at last they landed on the moon.

"There's nobody here," said Baby Bear.
"There are no trees," said the owl.
"It's a bit boring," said Baby Bear.
"Shall we have a picnic?"
"What a good idea," said the owl.

"We'd better go," said Baby Bear.
"My bath must be ready by now."
Off they went, down and down.
The owl got out and flew away.
"Goodbye," he said. "It was so nice
to meet you."

It rained and
the rain dripped through
Baby Bear's helmet.

Home went Baby Bear.
Back down the chimney
and on to the living room carpet
with a BUMP!

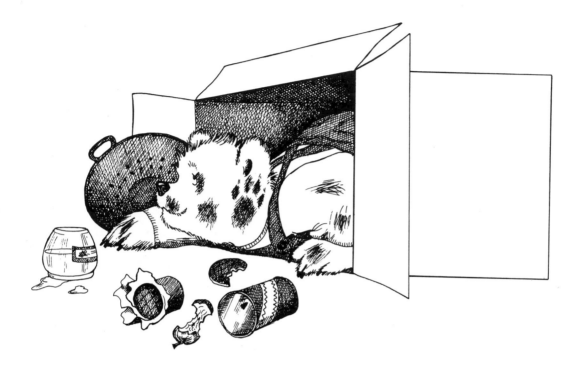

Mrs Bear came into the room.
"Look at the *state* of you!" she gasped
as she led him away to the bathroom.
"Why, you look as if you've been up the chimney."

"As a matter of fact," said Baby Bear,
"I *have* been up the chimney.
I found a rocket and went to
visit the moon."
Mrs Bear laughed.
"You and your stories," she said.
"Whatever next?"